MATTA NAPKIN

A DAILY COMIC... ON A NAPKIN... IN A BOOK

ODD CHARM PRESS

ODD CHARM PRESS
MATTA NAPKIN

COPYRIGHT @ 2015 JOHN MATTA

EDITOR: ROSE ABDOO
LAYOUT: EVA CRAWFORD
COVER PHOTOGRAPHY: CHRIS HASTON
TRAY PHOTOGRAPHY: DAVE KOGA

ISBN: 978-0-69238860-0

WHY ARE YOU READING THIS STUFF?

FINALLY, A SPLENDID BOOK OF NAPKIN ART BY THE NAPKIN
ARTIST OF THE CENTURY!!
    –NIA VARDALOS

THIS BOOK WILL WARM YOUR HEART. IF YOU LIGHT IT ON
FIRE AND PUT IT ON YOUR CHEST.
    –ERIC STONESTREET

JOHN PROVES THAT NAPKIN ARTISTRY IS VALUABLE TO
THOSE WHO LIKE TO USE ART TO CLEAN THEIR FACE
AFTER EATING. BUY THIS BOOK AND GET A SANDWICH.
    –JEFF GARLIN

WHY?
    –MARTIN SHORT

IT ALL STARTED WHEN I DREW A CARTOON ON A NAPKIN
FOR MY WIFE, ROSE. SINCE I'D NEVER REALLY DRAWN
BEFORE, SHE WAS DELIGHTED.

EVENTUALLY, I EXHAUSTED ROSE BY SHOWING HER DAILY
NAPKINS. SHE SAID, "I THINK YOU SHOULD SHOW THESE
TO OTHER PEOPLE BESIDES ME." SO I PUT THEM ON
THE WEB.

FOUR YEARS AND OVER NINE HUNDRED NAPKINS
LATER... NOW IT'S A BOOK.

I HOPE YOU LIKE IT.

MATTA

HOW MANY WRONGS MAKE A RIGHT?

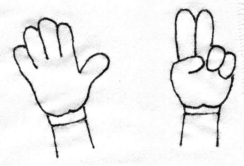

GROWING PARANOIA

THERE ARE TWO REASONS WHY I DON'T DO PUSH-UPS IN PUBLIC.
1. I CANNOT DO A PUSH-UP.
2.

I THINK THE VOICES IN MY HEAD MOVED...
BUT I CAN STILL HEAR SOMEONE WALKING
AROUND.

WHY DIDN'T PIRATES FINISH OFF THEIR PEG LEG WITH A WHEEL?

I'M NOT A FAN OF POST-IT-NOTES TOILET PAPER.

A VELVET CAPE IS MORE OF A THIRD DATE THING.

WOULDN'T IT BE TREMENDOUS IF THE SECRETARY OF ENERGY LOOKED LIKE THIS?

WEIGHT WISE... I JUST DON'T WANT MY PICTURE APPEARING IN ANY MEDICAL TEXT BOOKS.

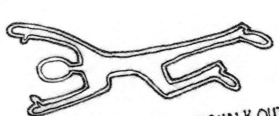

HOW MUCH I WEIGH IN MAJOR LEAGUE BASEBALLS

WHAT DOESN'T KILL YOU WILL PROBABLY TASTE GOOD WASHED DOWN WITH A COKE ZERO.

I JUST WANT TO LEAVE A THIN CHALK OUTLINE.

I MISTAKENLY SWALLOWED A SELF-ADHESIVE STAMP. NOW I CAN'T LOOK AT MYSELF IN THE MIRROR.

UNLESS YOU'RE STEALING FROM YOU'RE JOB, THERE'S NO REASON FOR AN ADULT TO CARRY A BACKPACK.

ALL MY EXIT INTERVIEWS END THE SAME... CRYING WITH A TRUNK FULL OF PENS AND LEGAL ENVELOPES.

I GOT FIRED AS A BATHROOM ATTENDANT FOR CONSTANTLY YELLING, "THAT'S ONE SWEET RIDE!"

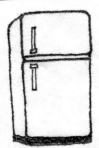

LISTEN, SHE TURNED YOU DOWN... CRYOGENICALLY FREEZING YOURSELF SO YOU CAN HAVE A SHOT AT HER DAUGHTER ISN'T A GOOD PLAN.

AT WHAT AGE DO YOU BUY STUFF THAT YOU KNOW YOU'RE GOING TO DIE OWNING?

HEADSTONE DESIGN #5

DEAR HIGH SCHOOL KIDS, DON'T MAKE A BABY ON TOP OF ME.

MATTA
1964 - 2170

COMAPALOOZA

I REALLY SHOULD HAVE LOST SOME WEIGHT BEFORE BUYING A DIAMOND FANNY PACK.

SO, IF YOU MEET A FUTURE VERSION OF YOURSELF DO YOU SHAKE HANDS? I'VE WRITTEN ALOT OF SCIENTISTS AND ETIQUETTE EXPERTS BUT NO REPLY.

YOU THINK YOU HAD A TOUGH DAY... TRY PUTTING A TUX ON A CHIMPANZEE FOR A ZOO WEDDING PARTY.

UNCOOL MOVE #23

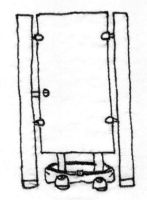

HUMMING POP GOES THE WEASEL IN A PUBLIC RESTROOM.

DARWIN CRUISING FOR LADIES

SO... ARE YOU UP FOR SOME SELECTIVE BREEDING?

MY WITCH DOCTOR MUST BE GETTING SOME KIND OF KICKBACK BECAUSE HE <u>ALWAYS</u> PRESCRIBES MONKEY PAW.

JUST BECAUSE YOU'RE 83 DOESN'T MEAN IT'S TOO LATE FOR BRACES!
– DR. IRA KREITMAN
OCTOGENARIAN ORTHODONTIST

MEDICARE ACCEPTED

AARP DISCOUNT

BAD BUS SIGN #8

ZOMBIE DIETICIAN ANNOUNCES CONTROVERSIAL SPINAL FLUID FAST.

CANNIBALS NEVER DEEP FRY... DO YOU THINK THEY KNOW SOMETHING WE DON'T?

MAYBE BEN'S LAWYER SHOULDN'T HAVE DUMPED GATORADE ON HIM WHEN HE WON THE INDECENT EXPOSURE CASE.

WAKING UP WITH A COCKROACH ON YOUR LIP ISN'T A KAFKAESQUE NIGHTMARE... IT'S A REASON NOT TO LEAVE PIZZA ON YOUR NIGHTSTAND.

GLASS HALF FULL... GLASS HALF EMPTY... CAN WE JUST AGREE TO GET THE URINE OFF THE TABLE?

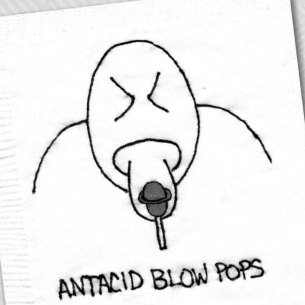

ANTACID BLOW POPS

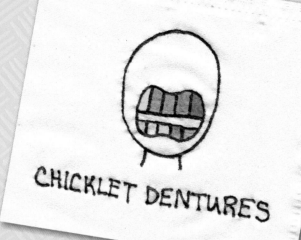

CHICKLET DENTURES

HORSE-FURKEY

REMOTE COLLAR

9

THANKS TO THE COPS MY TRI-STATE SANDWICH EATING SPREE ENDED THIS MORNING.

I SPENT 18 MINUTES SHAKING PRINGLES TO FIND THE PERFECT CAN... I STILL REGRET MY CHOICE.

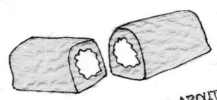

THERE IS JUST SOMETHING ABOUT MY 60 OZ TWINKIE DREAM THAT MAKES ME WISH I COULD GET INTO A COMA.

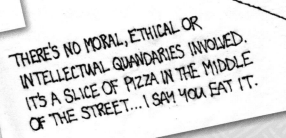

THERE'S NO MORAL, ETHICAL OR INTELLECTUAL QUANDARIES INVOLVED. IT'S A SLICE OF PIZZA IN THE MIDDLE OF THE STREET... I SAY YOU EAT IT.

NEW JERSEY LOTTERY   DATE: AUGUST 29, 2013

PAY TO THE
ORDER OF AZZAREYA $ 800.00

EIGHT HUNDRED   DOLLARS

FOR: AFTERNOON DATE

EVEN IF YOU WIN THE LOTTERY YOU CAN'T
PAY FOR A HOOKER WITH AN OVERSIZED CHECK.

LIFE MISTAKE #48

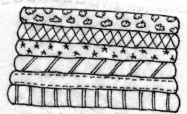

INVESTING IN THE DEATH BED MATTRESS STORE.
EVEN IF YOU GET THE BLOOD OUT... PEOPLE
STILL WANT A NAME BRAND.

MY FAVORITE THING ABOUT ARCHITECTURE IS IMAGINING HOW MANY
"MISSISSIPPIS" IT WOULD TAKE TO FALL FROM A BUILDING TO THE
SIDEWALK.

THERE'S A LOT WORSE THINGS TO BE CALLED IN
PRISON THAN, "BLANKET HOG."

NO, IT DOESN'T MENTION 32 HEALTHY TEETH IN THE BIBLE. I'M GUESSING THEY WERE HOPING YOU'D FIGURE OUT A COUPLE THINGS FOR YOURSELF.

MY DENTIST JUST REFERRED TO MY TEETH AS "HIGHLY UNSTABLE". THAT'S GOOD, RIGHT?

WHENEVER MY THERAPIST MAKES A NOTE HE HUMS CALLIOPE MUSIC.

MY DOCTOR HATES THAT I MAKE HIM WEAR THE MIRROR THING ON HIS HEAD... BUT I WANT THE WHOLE MAGILLA.

MY FAST FOOD LAWSUIT BARELY FITS.

MY DOCTOR SAID MY COLONOSCOPY LOOKED LIKE AN EPISODE OF HOARDERS. THAT'S GOOD, RIGHT?

THAT LIQUID NITROGEN BARBER REALLY DID A NUMBER ON ME.

YOU CAN'T ADD "FUN DAY" TO YOUR 7 DAY PILL CASE.

JOHN HANCOCK ALSO SIGNED SYMPATHY CARDS LIKE A JERK OFF.

OUR PRAYERS ARE WITH YOU

John Hancock

APRIL 2, 2053

LINCOLN MEETS SLASH IN HEAVEN

UNLESS IT'S ABRAHAM LINCOLN **DON'T** TRUST A MAN WITH A STOVEPIPE HAT IN HIS LAP.

I BET THAT BEARD ON THE BACK OF HER NECK EVERY NIGHT IS WHAT DROVE MARY TODD LINCOLN NUTS.

IT CREEPS THE LADIES OUT WHEN YOU OVER PRONOUNCE EVERY SYLLABLE OF THE WORD, "MOISTURIZER."

WHENEVER ANYONE MAKES FUN OF MY TINY BABY EARS I ALWAYS BLAME, "A TIME TRAVEL ACCIDENT."

SPEED DATING? I BETTER GET FRESH BATTERIES FOR MY HYPNO-SOMBRERO.

DATING TIP #9

EVEN IF IT'S REALLY SWANKY DON'T INVITE A LADY BACK TO YOUR CUSHION FORT.

BAD PRE-SEX TALK

"NICE SHEETS...I BET THOSE WOULD MAKE
A GREAT ESCAPE ROPE."

MOUSTACHE RIDE

ES SELDOM SAY "..."

FIRST DATE TIP #37

PUT YOUR STUFFED ANIMAL COLLECTION IN THE CLOSET
UNTIL YOU "CLOSE THE DEAL."

YOU CAN'T PAY FOR A FALAFEL WITH RAW SENSUALITY... OR CAN YOU?

I WAS A LITTLE WORRIED ABOUT WEARING A SUIT FROM STEVE HARVEY'S "LADIES OF THE WNBA COLLECTION" BUT I THINK I PULLED IT OFF.

SHARK WEEK MEETS FASHION WEEK

FORMAL SEX DOES NOT REQUIRE A TUXEDO... IT DOES HOWEVER REQUIRE 300 DOLLARS.

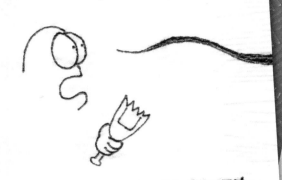

I CAN'T BELIEVE I BROUGHT A BROKEN BOTTLE TO A BULLWHIP FIGHT. I SHOULD HAVE READ THE ENTIRE EVITE.

MY QUILL AT STARBUCKS GOT ME VERY LITTLE POSITIVE ATTENTION.

YOU CAN'T BRING BACK A LOVED ONE... BUT A SHOVEL WILL HELP YOU GET THAT RING BACK.

TODAY I PROVED ONE MAN WITH A BUCKET OF ROCKS AND A TENNIS RACKET CAN MAKE A DIFFERENCE.

EVER WONDER WHAT YOUR LIFE WOULD BE LIKE IF YOUR PARENTS STUDIED HARDER IN HIGH SCHOOL?

WHEN MY PARENTS BROUGHT MY LITTLE BROTHER HOME THEY SHOULDN'T HAVE INTRODUCED HIM AS "MY REPLACEMENT."

THE BEST THING ABOUT BEING AN UNCLE: I DON'T GIVE A SHIT IF YOU DON'T SMILE ALL DAY.

FAVORITE CHILDHOOD MEMORY #6

READING THE FLYPAPER WITH MY DAD

NO ONE THINKS "THE OLD SWITCHEROO" IS FUNNY AT THE MATERNITY WARD.

I THINK IT'S VERY BRAVE THAT ALAN AND MARK DECIDED TO BECOME SIAMESE TWINS LATER IN LIFE.

I DON'T CONSIDER IT "LIFE" UNTIL IT CAN SLAM DUNK.

I'M REALLY SURPRISED MY MOM AGREED TO A SHOT-FOR-SHOT REMAKE OF MY BIRTH VIDEO.

EATING A PIE IN A CLOSET...MY THIRD FAVORITE BIRTHDAY MEMORY.

IF I HAD A PREHENSILE TAIL... I THINK I'D WEAR A WATCH MORE.

I JUST GOT A CALL FROM MYSELF IN A PARALLEL UNIVERSE AND WE BOTH APOLOGIZED.

I WAS IN A PAN FLUTE GARAGE BAND.

CLOWN NOSE SWEAT SHOP

BAD IDEAS TO TURN INTO LAMPS:

E.P.T. LAMP

THE SKULL OF BOB CRANE LAMP

KNIFE LAMP

CHOCOLATE BUNNY LAMP

TURKEY JERKY LAMP

IHOP SYRUP LAMP

COLUMBIAN NECKTIES

OPEN 9-5

EVEN THOUGH PEOPLE WERE TOO AFRAID TO COME INSIDE, EDUARDO REFUSED TO RENAME HIS STORE.

THAT VAGISIL FACTORY JUST WON'T STOP BURNING.

THE LADIES AT THE NAIL PLACE ACTED LIKE THEY'VE NEVER SEEN A STIGMATA.

MY FAVORITE SAINT HAS ALWAYS BEEN ST. STEVE... THE PATRON SAINT OF LEANING ON THE HORN.

I THOUGHT MEGAPHONE CONFESSION WOULD BE FUN... UNTIL WE GOT TO THE MEATY PART.

GODZILLA BAR MITZVAH

MATTA-VENTION #63

BALLSWEAT BANDS

EASTER ISLAND BONNET

MATTA-VENTION #43

THE I'M WITH STUPID DIAPHRAGM

MATTA-VENTION #15

← SHIRT

← EYE GLASS WIPE

THE RUB HEM

CHIPPENDALES BABY

STROLLER WARS

THERE'S NOTHING WORSE THAN MISTAKENLY
BUYING A TICKET TO THE MOMMY AND ME
MATINEE AT THE ADULT THEATRE.

HOW NOT TO WRAP A BABY SHOWER GIFT.

DEAR MOM,
SCREAM WHISPER ALL YOU WANT... I'M
NOT GOING TO PUT MY SHOES BACK ON
IN CHURCH.
Love,
Matte
(YOUR SON)

YOU SHOULDN'T OWN A "CHURCH MIDRIFF."

DON'T BEAT BOX IN CONFESSION.

I'M HALFWAY THROUGH BUT IF SOME DRACULAS
DON'T SHOW UP SOON... I'M DONE WITH THE
BIBLE.

SURE LIFE CAN BE ROUGH, BUT UNTIL YOU'RE WEARING A BIKINI AT A CAR SHOW DON'T COMPLAIN TO ME.

I'M NEVER SURE WHICH TASTES WORST... THE VOLTS OR AMPS.

I JUST DON'T HAVE THE JAWLINE FOR A JELLY BEAN GOATEE.

BAKE THE CAKE FIRST BEFORE ADDING THE GIRL.

INTERVIEW MISTAKE #89

WHEN ASKED YOUR BIGGEST WEAKNESS
DON'T REPLY, "VODKA SOURS."

JESUS LOVES HIS PEEPS

LIFE IMITATES ART WHEN I'M
NAILED TO A WALL.

GAME DAY AT THE MORGUE

OKAY, I ATE THE OBESITY REPORT... ARE YOU HAPPY?

KISSING THAT STREET CAT WAS A REMARKABLE LAPSE OF GOOD JUDGEMENT ON MY PART.

IT KINDA SUCKS MY EVIL TWIN CAN GROW A MOUSTACHE AND I CAN'T.

DON'T STALK A KENYAN MARATHON RUNNER... THAT'S HOW I GOT PLANTAR FACIITIS.

MY BODY IS A TEMPLE FOR ABOUT 40 LITTLE FAT GUYS.

WHEN THE CLONE WARS HAPPEN, I WANT TO GET IN EARLY AND FIGHT MYSELF AS A BABY.

THE STARS MIGHT HOLD THE SECRETS OF CREATION BUT I KNOW HOW TO EAT A TACO WITHOUT TIPPING MY HEAD SIDEWAYS.

THE VOICES IN MY HEAD JUST GOT MAR DO I HAVE TO SEND THEM A GIFT?

SHARK WEEK
vs
SECRETARY WEEK

PIZZA DAY AT THE MORGUE

The Running Of The Kitties
At
La Fiesta De Los Gatos

Goldfish
Key Party

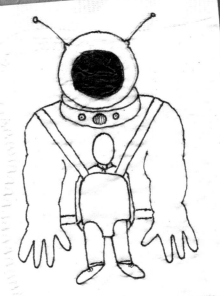

HOW I'D LIKE TO GET TO WORK.

"EVEN IF I HAD A MAGIC WAND I WOULDN'T CHANGE THE PART IN MY HAIR."

— THE 3RD MOST EMBARRASSING THING I'VE SAID ALOUD.

DID ANYONE CONSIDER THE THEORY THAT RIP VAN WINKLE MIGHT HAVE BEEN IN A COMA?

TOOTH FAIRY ROAD KILL

I CAN'T HELP BUT LAUGH WHENEVER I HEAR THE FRANKESTEIN MONSTER DESCRIBE HIMSELF AS A, "SELF-MADE MAN."

AMERICAN INDIAN SERIAL KILLERS...

... USE EVERY SINGLE PART OF THE HITCHHIKER.

ALWAYS GET THE EXTENDED WARRANTY ON THE ARTIFICIAL HEART.

AS THE ANESTHESIOLOGIST PUT ME TO SLEEP HE WHISPERED, "THEY'RE GOING TO PEEL YOU LIKE A GRAPE."

BETWEEN THE COMA AND NOT TAKING OUT THE WHITE STRIPS DON HAS A BREATHTAKING SMILE.

DON IS TOTALLY UP FOR SOME WORKSPACE ROMANCE AT THE TOLL BOOTH.

EVEN THOUGH ALL THE GROOMSMEN CHEERED, DON SHOULDN'T HAVE LIT HIS FART WITH THE FLAME OF THE UNITY CANDLE.

AFTER 12 YEARS DON JUST GOT BURNED OUT BY THE BUTTON DOWN WORLD OF COCK FIGHTING.

WHAT I SEE LOOKING BACK AT ME EVERY MORNING.

YOU REALLY CAN'T PRACTICE CPR IN A MIRROR.

MATTA-VENTION #143

BUBBLE WRAP HEADBAND

DON'T WRITE YOUR SUICIDE NOTE IN BINARY. IT JUST COMPLICATES EVERYTHING.

FATHER DAUGHTER DAY AT THE SIDESHOW

INTERVIEW MISTAKE #44

UNDER SPECIAL SKILLS YOU SHOULDN'T WRITE, "TEACHING BABIES TO CURSE."

DADDY DAUGHTER DAY AT THE MORGUE

I'M THINKING ABOUT OUTSOURCING MY WEEKLY CALL TO MY PARENTS.

THE TIEKIN

MY DAVID LEE IRA ROTH ISN'T MATURING VERY WELL.

A THRONE OF SKULLS IS AWESOME...A BEAN BAG CHAIR OF SKULLS IS UNCOMFORTABLE.

THAT LEGO PROSTATE EXAM KIT IS A LITTLE CREEPY.

WHAT I LEARNED FROM THE SHOW LOCKUP.

JUST BECAUSE HE STOPPED THE ARYAN BROTHERHOOD FROM BRUTALIZING YOU, DOESN'T MEAN HE'S "THE ONE."

LAWN ORNAMENT MIXED MARRIAGE

YOU ARE A JERK OFF... GET OUT OF MY LIFE!

PUBLISHERS CLEARING HOUSE BREAK UP NOTE

SOUNDING OUT THE HARD WORDS ISN'T THE IDEAL WAY TO READ YOUR WEDDING VOWS.

TODAY WE HONOR ALL THE BRAVE MEN AND WOMEN SLAIN WHILE SERVING THE RODEO INDUSTRY.

UPS WEDDING

PICTURE DAY AT THE MAD SCIENTIST DAY CARE

HELMET TESTERS RETIREMENT DINNER

CLONE DISCIPLINE

ABSENT MINDED SERIAL KILLER

CARNIVAL BABY

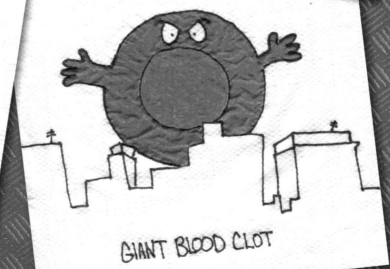

GIANT BLOOD CLOT

I FELL DOWN A WELL AND MY DOG DIDN'T DO SHIT.

THE VOICES IN MY HEAD JUST GOT A DOG. NOW HOW ARE THEY GOING TO GO AWAY ON WEEKENDS?

I WAS REALLY HOPING THIS WAS GOING TO BE ONE OF THOSE COOL CHARLOTTE'S WEB SPIDERS... INSTEAD IT JUST STARES AT ME.

I DON'T THINK MY CAT WILL EVER FORGIVE ME FOR ONLY POSTING $25 AS A REWARD.

I HAVE A CELEBRITY DEATH POOL IN THE SHAPE OF ARTIE LANGE.

LOST IN SPACE RODEO

DEATH TAKES A HOLIDAY

MY LIFE'S BIGGEST DREAM

TO REMAKE THE ZAPRUDER FILM WITH MONKEYS.

42

It's been 47 years, I can't believe my parents are still living with me.

THE HUNCHBACK OF NOTRE DAD

IS THERE ANY PAINT FROM CHINA MY KID CAN EAT?

4TH OF JULY BABY

JULY 4, 2013

INSTEAD OF "OOHING AND AAHING" AT FIREWORKS I LIKE TO YELL, "HAS ANYONE SEEN MY SEIZURE MEDICINE?!"

I LIKE KIDS, BUT EVEN MINE AGREE I SHOULDN'T HAVE ANY OF MY OWN.

IF INSTEAD OF THAT STUPID BALL THEY USED A CLEAR BAG OF EYEBALLS... SOCCER WOULD INSTANTLY BECOME MORE POPULAR IN AMERICA.

I'VE ALWAYS WANTED TO WORK WITH CHILDREN... ONES THAT KNOW HOW TO MAKE iPHONES.

DON'T EVER GET HIGH AND BEAD YOUR CAT'S HAIR.

CLOUD SEX PARTY

SUICIDE PACT SELFIE

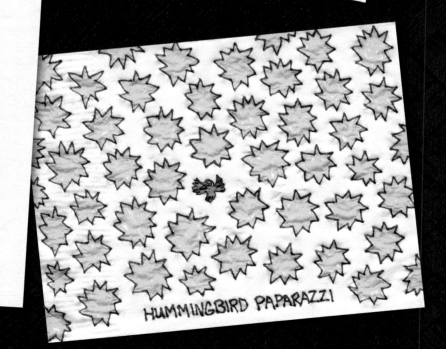

HUMMINGBIRD PAPARAZZI

THAT'S NOT HOW YOU CHILDPROOF A GUN.

THAT LEPROSY FUN RUN WAS LIKE A MINE FIELD.

NO ONE LIKES A BAD WINNER AT THE RUSSIAN ROULETTE TABLE.

LEROY NEIMAN CRIME SCENE

I'VE COMMITTED 3 OF THE 7 DEADLY SINS AND I STILL SLEEP LIKE A BABY.

A LITTLE BIRD TOLD ME THAT I'M GOING TO COME INTO SOME MONEY... THEN I'M GOING TO BE MURDERED. WHAT A SHITTY LITTLE BIRD.

I REALLY THOUGHT HAVING A 3RD NIPPLE WOULD BE A GREAT ICEBREAKER WITH THE LADIES AT THE BEACH.

ONE MAN CAN TRULY MAKE A DIFFERENCE... ESPECIALLY IF HE TELLS THAT COUPLE TO TAKE THEIR BABY OUT OF THE MOVIE THEATER.

MY MOTHER AND I LOVED THE COSTCO PARKING LOT IN AUGUST. IT WAS PERFECT FOR MAKING TAR ANGELS.

MY UNCLE KEN IS A RACIST. I MEAN... CIVIL WAR BUFF.

WHENEVER MY GRANDFATHER FINISHED A POPSICKLE HE'D HAND ME THE STICK AND YELL, "HERE'S ANOTHER HAMPSTER TOMBSTONE!"

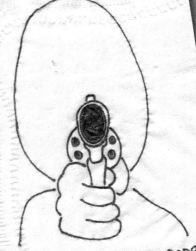

MY UNCLE DON WAS A DOOR-TO-DOOR GUN SALESMAN. HE REALLY SHOULD'VE USED A BRIEFCASE.

THE NEW POPE BETTER CONTROL HIS PEOPLE...I HAD TO GO TO TEN DIFFERENT CONFESSIONALS BEFORE I GOT A DEAL.

IF I WERE GOD, YELLOW WOULD HAVE BEEN MY FIRST COLOR CHOICE FOR BLOOD.

YESTERDAY POPE FRANCIS AND FORMER POPE BENEDICT XVI MET FOR LUNCH.

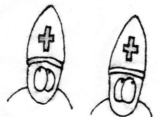

IT WAS A HISTORIC MEAL UNTIL THE CHECK ARRIVED... THEN IT GOT WEIRD.

FOR A "WIZARD" HE REALLY MAKES A SHITTY PATTY MELT.

WITH ONLY ONE COYOTE CUSTOMER, THE QUALITY CONTROL AT ACME EXPLOSIVES CONTINUED TO SLIP.

MOUSE TO MOUSE RESUSCITATION

MORE BODIES WERE FOUND THIS EVENING RAISING THE ROACH MOTEL DEATH TOLL TO 80.

WHEN HE'S NOT AROUND 10,247 OF HIS WORKER BUDDIES, THE KILLER BEE REALLY ISN'T THAT SCARY.

51

SURVIVOR'S GUILT

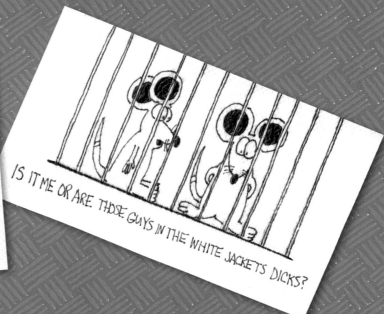

IS IT ME OR ARE THOSE GUYS IN THE WHITE JACKETS DICKS?

SIAMESE TWINS DON'T ALWAYS AGREE.

LIFE IS LIKE A BOWL OF CHERRIES...
IT'S SLOWLY BEING DESTROYED BY
MONSANTO.

A CANDLE LIGHT VIGIL FOR THE VICTIMS OF THE CANDLE STORE MASSACRE.

ANTI-DEODORANT LOBBY

IT MIGHT BE CALLED THE OPTIMIST CLUB BUT IF YOU DON'T POUR TO THE RIM THEY LOSE THEIR SHIT.

CLONE ROAST

AT LEAST I WASN'T MADE FROM A SINGLE LOCK OF HAIR LIKE YOU JAGOFFS.

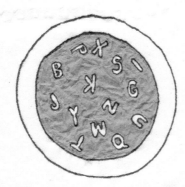

DOES ANYONE KNOW WHAT FONT THEY USE IN ALPHABET SOUP?

DEAR GOATEES,

ARE YOU ABOUT DONE?

Love,

Matha

IF I LISTENED TO EVERYBODY I WOULDN'T HAVE THESE SWEET PROSTHETIC OSTRICH LEGS. #LISTENTOYOURHEART

FOR A MILLION DOLLAR RACE HORSE... THERE WASN'T A LOT OF MEAT.

IT'S NOT EASY SITTING THROUGH A MURDER TRIAL WHEN YOU'VE GOT ÉCLAIRS AT HOME.

SMOKEY'S SECOND JOB

FOR AN EXTRA TEN BUCKS I'LL SHOW YOU AN INDIAN GRAVEYARD.

RABBI FRANKENSTEIN SCOURS THE TORAH SEEKING REDEMPTION FOR THROWING THAT LITTLE GIRL IN THE LAKE.

THE THOUSAND YARD STARE OF AN ADULT THEATER JANITOR.

WONDERFUL
WOULDN'T IT BE HORRIBLE IF THE MAIN INGREDIENT IN VIAGRA WAS BABY TEARS?

REMEMBER AT THE BABY SHOWER CALL IT A BABY... NOT A PARASITIC TENANT.

YOU SHOULD NEVER DESCRIBE YOURSELF AS "THE TOP GUN OF GYNECOLOGISTS."

I THINK THE VOICES IN MY HEAD WENT THROUGH WITH THE SUICIDE PACT. I HAVEN'T HEARD ANYTHING FOR DAYS AND THE SMELL IS OVERWHELMING.

DODGEBALL SELFIE

A HIGH-FIVERS NIGHTMARE

THE BABY TOOTHED SHARK

BOTOXED BOZO

DON THOUGHT SECRETLY GIVING THE FINGER IN ALL HIS WEDDING PHOTOS WOULD BE SOMETHING THEY COULD LAUGH AT FOR YEARS TO COME.

I SAY IT'S OKAY TO GO TO BED ANGRY BECAUSE THEN YOU CAN GET SOME SHARPIE JUSTICE.

THEY MET ON TINDER

IF YOU GET DIVORCED BEFORE YOUR FIRST YEAR ANNIVERSARY YOU SHOULD BOTH BE REQUIRED TO SWALLOW YOUR WEDDING RINGS.

CASUALLY MENTIONING YOUR AERODYNAMIC SPERM
ISN'T A WAY TO GET OUT OF JURY DUTY.

I JUST PRAY MY DEATHBED
ISN'T ON MILK CRATES.

ETIQUETTE WISE... AFTER A PLANE CRASH WHAT'S
THE ACCEPTABLE PERIOD TO WAIT BEFORE YOU
START EATING EACH OTHER?

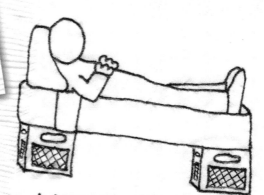

I ALWAYS KEEP A FIFTY DOLLAR BILL IN MY SHOE. IN CASE I
DIE IT'LL CHEER UP THE FOLKS WHO FIND MY BODY.

LEPROSY LEOPARD

A BORN SHOWMAN

WEDDING VOWS SHOULD NEVER BE DESCRIBED AS "FIENDISH."

BABY DRACULA

IF YOU RUN OUT OF CANDY DON'T GIVE OUT MINESTRONE.

MY WORST HALLOWEEN MEMORY:

THE YEAR MY CHEAP DAD MADE ME GO AS A DUCT TAPE MUMMY.

WHAT DO YOU CARE IF I'M GLUTEN FREE?

HAPPY HALLOWEEN

SIAMESE GHOST TWINS

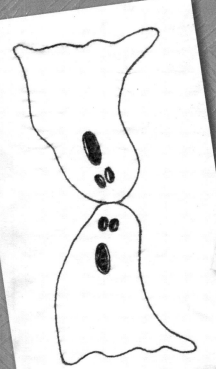

THE GHOSTS OF STATIC CLING

HOLDING UP A GUN AND A CANDY BAR ISN'T A GOOD WAY TO ILLUSTRATE, "TRICK OR TREAT" TO CHILDREN.

DYSLEXIC GHOST

OOB!

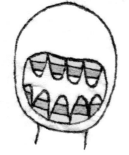

HALLOWEEN GRILL

I LEARNED I CAN'T RUN AWAY FROM MY PROBLEMS...
AT LEAST NOT UNTIL I GET IN SHAPE.

ALPHABET SOUP SUICIDE NOTE

...HT I HEARD A DOZEN DOGS
...WUT BUTTER.

AS A KID NO ONE BELIEVED I'D SET THE WORLD ON FIRE...
BUT I DID GET TO BURN DOWN THE HIGH SCHOOL.

JUMBO PENCILS DO NOT LIGHTEN THE MOOD WHEN FILLING OUT DEATH CERTIFICATES.

OCEAN COUNTY
DEPARTMENT OF JUSTICE

GETTING ARRESTED WOULD BE SO MUCH MORE FUN IF THEY FINGERPRINTED WITH CHEETOS INSTEAD OF INK.

WHY DOESN'T THIS EXIST?

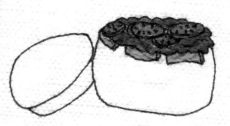

THE BREAD BOWL SANDWICH

I THINK THE VOICES IN MY HEAD ARE BECOMING PARANOID... WHENEVER I PICK UP THE PHONE THEY TELL ME THEY HEAR VOICES.

64

MR. PEANUT DISCOVERING HE'S ALLERGIC TO HIMSELF.

EVEN THE SPERM BANK IS GOING GREEN.

UNTIL THE SURGERY, MAKO SAID HE ALWAYS FELT LIKE A SHARK TRAPPED IN A GOLDFISH BODY.

THERE IS NOTHING SADDER THAN WHEN THEY HAVE TO CUT THE RAT OUT OF THE CAGE AT THE OBESITY STUDY LAB.

THE TRAP DOOR FACTORY WAS ODDLY QUIET.

"WHO TOOK A SHIT IN THE CURSE JAR?"
— THE THIRD WORST THING SAID
IN MY HOME GROWING UP.

GROWING UP WE HAD 5 GOLDFISH DIE IN THE
LIVING ROOM AND NO ONE BUT ME SAW THE
IRONY.

"YOU'D BE SURPRISED HOW MUCH ASS I GET FROM
THE OBITUARY SECTION."
— THE 3RD WORST THING MY UNCLE KEN
SAID ALOUD.

WILLIAM TELL'S SON'S OPEN CASKET

SUPERFAN FUNERAL

FARTING PALLBEARER

FUNERAL HOME TIP #12

DON'T PUT THE DELI PLATES ON THE OPEN CASKET.

I NEED TO EXERCISE LESS PATIENCE AND EXERCISE MORE EXERCISE.

WHENEVER I MEET A CAT THE FIRST THING I CONTEMPLATE IS IF I CAN BEAT IT IN HAND-TO-PAW COMBAT. SO FAR I'VE ONLY BEEN WRONG THREE TIMES.

I KNOW THIS SOUNDS CRAZY BUT I THINK MY STROBE READING LAMP IS GIVING ME A MIGRANE.

I THINK MY DOG IS STARTING TO HEAR THE VOICES IN MY HEAD... OUT OF NOWHERE HE'LL JUST SIT.

I'VE BEEN DRINKING MERCURY ALL WEEK... IF I GOTTA GO I'M TAKING PEOPLE WITH ME.

HAPPY THANKSGIVING FROM THE MONSANTO FAMILY

THE CRANBERRY TOWER INFERNO

CAN WE GO BACK TO TURKEY NEXT YEAR?

HAPPY THANKSGIVING

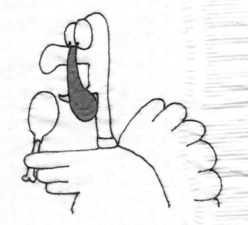

TURKEY CANNIBAL

THAT INSIDE-OUT TURKEY REALLY MADE THE KIDS TABLE CRY.

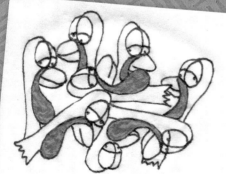

WHERE DO YOU THINK BUTTERBALL PUTS ALL THE HEADS?

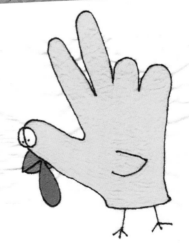

SHOP TEACHER HAND TURKEY

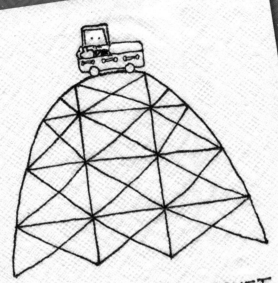

ROLLER COASTER OPEN CASKET

HYDROCEPHALUS
SNOWMAN

NO, I'M GOOD.

ARE YOU SURE YOU
DON'T WANT TO DIVIDE?

CELL TALK

SNAKENECK

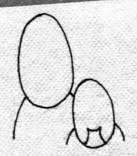

MAYBE IT'S A GROSS STEREOTYPE BUT I FEEL ALOT OF VENTRILOQUIST DUMMIES ARE INCREDIBLY RUDE.

VENTRILOQUISTS IN LOVE

THE SAD TRUTH WAS DON ALWAYS HAD A TOOTHACHE... HE WASN'T JUST A CRAPPY VENTRILOQUIST.

VENTRILOQUIST GIRL'S NIGHT OUT

IF TODAY'S YOUTH SICKEN YOU SO MUCH...WHY DO YOU KEEP EATING THEM?
— CANNIBAL QUANDARY

CAN BEEF JERKY GO BAD IN YOUR CHEEKS? PLEASE LET ME KNOW BY FRIDAY.

I'VE NEVER GOTTEN IT IN A HUMAN'S MOUTH BUT IT HASN'T BEEN FOR A LACK OF TRYING.

WHY DOESN'T THIS EXIST?

GOOGLY EYE BOXERS

BRUSH ALL YOU WANT, YOUR TEETH ARE STILL GOING TO FALL OUT IN YOUR DREAMS.

WHEN I WAS SEVEN AND FOUND OUT YOU COULD JUST BUY SHEETS OF GOLD STARS... A LITTLE BIT OF MY CHILDHOOD SLIPPED AWAY.

PEOPLE ASK ME HOW I LOST 100 POUNDS. THE TRICK IS... FIRST PUT ON 100 POUNDS... THEN WORK BACKWARDS.

PEOPLE TELL YOU NOT TO EAT THE YELLOW SNOW... BUT THE BROWN SNOW IS JUST REVOLTING.

SONNY CORLEONE-MAN

DUE TO BUDGET CUTBACKS EVERY SNOWFLAKE WILL BE THE SAME.

— THE MANAGEMENT

ALMOST 50 YEARS ON THE PLANET AND SANTA HAS YET TO BRING ME A CHIMPANZEE... DOESN'T THE GUY READ HIS MAIL?

RUDOLPH SMOKING IN A SNOW STORM.

ALL THESE YEARS AND NO ONE KNEW SANTA WAS SPORTING LOBSTER BOY HANDS UNDER HIS MITTENS.

SANTA IS A STICKLER ABOUT WATER CONSERVATION.

TAKE 10 DAYS OF ZITHROMAX AND YOU SHOULD BE ABLE TO FLY BY THE 24TH.

MERRY CHRISTMAS FROM THE TOOTH FAIRY.

I'D LIKE TO THANK THE FOLLOWING PEOPLE WHO WITHOUT THEIR FRIENDSHIP AND HELP THIS BOOK WOULDN'T BE POSSIBLE.

CLAUDIA CARPENTER	LESLEY HERSHMAN
SEAN MURPHY	CHRIS HASTON
CRAIG DOYLE	DAVE RYGALSKI
NIA VARDALOS	NICK VARDALOS
KEN DALY	MIKE LATINO
SUZY NAKAMURA	ERIC STONESTREET
MACKLIN DWYER	BIL DWYER
MARK BANKER	CORE
MARK FITE	FIONA JORDAN
CHRIS MATTA	KATHY MATTA

AND FINALLY MY TWO FAVORITE PEOPLE... MIKE & MURIEL MATTA